The Baby Sister

written and illustrated by

Tomie dePaola

SCHOLASTIC INC.
New York Toronto London Auckland Sydney

For my sister, Maureen

ISBN 0-590-13843-X

12 11 10 9 8 7 6 5 4 3 2 1   7 8 9/9 0 1 2/0

Printed in the U.S.A.   09
First Scholastic printing, September 1997

Tommy had a mother, a father, two grandmothers, one grandfather, lots of aunts and uncles, an older brother, Buddy,
a dog named Tootsie…

...and lots and lots of cousins.

So when Tommy's mother told him that she was going to have a baby, Tommy said, "Can I have a baby sister with a red ribbon in her hair?"

"We'll see," his mother told him.

Tommy's family started getting the baby's room ready.
Dad and Buddy painted the walls white and the crib
a bright yellow.

Mom made new curtains and piled snow-white diapers and
baby clothes on the shelf above the baby's changing table.

"Can I do something for the baby's room?" Tommy asked his mother. "I want to paint a picture for the wall."

"Of course you can," his mother said.

Every night when Tommy said his prayers, he ended with, "Please, please, send me a baby sister with a red ribbon in her hair."

As the months passed, his mother's tummy grew bigger and bigger.

"The baby's in here," she told Tommy, pointing to her tummy. Tommy leaned his head against her. "Hi, baby," he whispered.

And when the baby began to move, his mother held Tommy's hand against her tummy. "Feel it?" she asked.

"It's kicking!" he answered.

"Soon I'll be going to the hospital, and then we'll know if you have a brother or a sister," his mother told him. "While I'm there Aunt Nell will come and take care of you."

Tommy smiled. He loved his Aunt Nell.

The next day, Tommy's Italian grandmother, Nana Fall-River, came for a visit from Fall River, where she lived.

"Guess what, Nana!" Tommy said. "I'm going to have a baby sister and she's in my mom's tummy just waiting to be born. And sometimes she kicks and I..."

"*Basta*, Tommasino—enough! I don't want to hear any more," she told him. Nana didn't think children should know all about babies and how they were born.

That night, when Tommy and Buddy were asleep, their mother told their dad that it was time to go to the hospital.

"Don't forget to wake up Tommy when you get home, Joe, and tell him if he has a new baby sister or a baby brother."

"I won't forget, Floss. I promise," Tommy's father said.

As soon as he got home, early in the morning, Tommy's dad woke him up. "You have a baby sister, Tommy."

"When can I see the baby! When can I see Mom! Are they coming home tomorrow?"

"Slow down, Tommy," his dad told him. "They have to stay at the hospital for a few days at least."

That night, Tommy asked when Aunt Nell was coming. "Well," his father answered, "since Nana's here, Aunt Nell won't be coming." Tommy's face fell. If he couldn't have his mother, he wanted Aunt Nell.

"*Mangia, mangia*, eat, eat, Tommasino. Your brother, Buddy, he eat up all nice," Nana said. She was always telling him what to do. She didn't like Tootsie in the house. And she was always talking to his dad in Italian, so Tommy couldn't understand them.

The next day, Tommy asked his dad if he could go see his mom. "I'm afraid not," Dad said. "Chicken pox is going around and you haven't had it yet, so they can't let you in the hospital right now."

The following day was even worse. Nana made him stay inside all afternoon just because it was raining a little. That night he wouldn't eat his dinner or do his homework. Tommy missed his mom so much.

On Friday, when school let out, Tommy heard a voice calling his name as he left the schoolyard. "Tommy, Tommy! Look up here. Up here." It was his mother, sitting at an open window in the hospital across the street.

"Mom!" Tommy shouted.

"You have a beautiful baby sister," his mom called down. "Now, you be a good boy, mind your Nana Fall-River, and I'll be home before you know it. All right?"

"I will, Mom. I will!" Tommy shouted.

When he got home, Nana was the only one there. "Nana, Nana,
I saw Mom. Up in the window!" Nana hugged him.
   "Let's be friends, Nana," he said, hugging her back.

At dinner Tommy ate every piece of spaghetti on his plate, and all the salad too.

On Sunday, his dad went to the hospital to get his mother and his baby sister. Everyone else waited at the house—Nana Fall-River and Nana his Irish grandmother; his grandfather, Tom; Uncle Charles and his girlfriend, Viva; Aunt Nell, Buddy, and Tootsie.

Tommy heard the car pull into the driveway. The door opened, and there was his mother, holding a small bundle in her arms. Tommy hid behind the big armchair as everybody crowded around his mom and the new baby.

"Where's Tommy?" his mother asked.

"Here I am!" Tommy shouted, jumping up from behind the armchair. "Here I am!"

His mom kissed him. Then Nana said, "*Firenze*, Florence, let Nana have the baby."

"My friend," Nana said, turning to Tommy, "sit down so you can hold your new sister."

Tommy sat in the big armchair. Nana placed the warm bundle
in his arms and folded back the blanket.

Tommy's baby sister, Maureen, with a red ribbon in her hair, looked up at him.

And Tommy was the happiest boy in the world.